Peter Pan

By J. M. Barrie

Adapted by Lucy Kincaid

Illustrated by Gill Guile

Brimax · Newmarket · England

Peter Pan

When Wendy, Michael and John are taught to fly by
Peter Pan, he takes them to the magical island of
Neverland. Here they meet the Lost Boys, the
Redskins and the terrible Captain Hook and his band
of pirates. Hook is desperate to capture Peter, and
will stop at nothing until this is done - even if it
means kidnapping Wendy!

Contents

Peter Breaks Through ———————————— 8

Come Away, Come Away ———————————— 10

The Flight ———————————————————— 15

The Island Come True ——————————— 17

The Mermaids' Lagoon ——————————— 24

The Never Bird ————————————————— 28

Wendy's Story ——————————————————— 29

Do You Believe in Fairies? ——————— 34

The Pirate Ship ————————————————— 37

The Return Home ————————————————— 41

When Wendy Grew Up ——————————————— 44

Peter Breaks Through

Wendy Darling and her brothers Michael and John had a nanny to look after them. This was not an ordinary nanny, but a Newfoundland dog called Nana.

One night when the children were in bed, Mrs. Darling was sewing in the nursery. She fell asleep and dreamed of a make-believe island called Neverland and a boy called Peter Pan.

As she slept, the nursery window opened and a boy flew in. With him was a strange light that flitted about the room. Mrs. Darling woke up. She knew the boy was Peter Pan.

Suddenly Nana rushed into the room. She sprang at the boy but he jumped onto the window sill and was gone. But the boy's shadow was left behind. It had caught on the window frame and was torn off. Mrs. Darling rolled it up and put it in a drawer.

Come Away, Come Away

A week later Mr. and Mrs. Darling went out, leaving Nana tied up in the backyard. The children were asleep in the nursery.

As the children slept, the night-lights went out and another light began moving around the room. It was Tinkerbell the fairy. She was helping Peter Pan look for his shadow.

Peter opened a drawer and found his shadow.
Then he shut the drawer with Tinkerbell still inside.
Peter tried to stick his shadow to his heels with a
piece of soap. It didn't work and he began to cry. His
sobs woke Wendy.

"I'll sew your shadow on for you," said Wendy to
Peter.

When Wendy had finished, Peter gave her an acorn button as a thank-you kiss. She put it on a chain around her neck. Peter told her he lived in Neverland with the Lost Boys.

"Who are the Lost Boys?" asked Wendy.

"Boys who fell out of their cradles when they were babies," said Peter. Then he told Wendy all about Neverland, and the pirates and redskins who lived there too.

Suddenly Peter remembered Tinkerbell, and he opened the drawer to let her out. She was very cross.

"I come to the nursery window to listen to the stories your mother tells you," said Peter. "The Lost Boys don't know any stories."

"I could tell them stories," said Wendy.

"I will teach you how to fly," said Peter. "Then you can come to Neverland with me."

By this time John and Michael were awake. They wanted to go to Neverland too. It sounded like an exciting place.

Meanwhile, Nana had escaped from the backyard and had gone to find Mr. and Mrs. Darling. She knew there was danger around. When she found them, they hurried home together. They saw four shadows circling around the nursery as Peter taught the children how to fly.

"Come!" cried Peter, and he flew out through the window. Wendy, John and Michael followed close behind him.

The Flight

"How do we get to Neverland?" asked Wendy.

"Second on the right and then straight on till morning," said Peter.

When they approached Neverland, they hid Tinkerbell in John's hat so that her light would not give them away to the pirates. They hated Peter Pan and the Lost Boys. But it was too late. The pirates had already seen them. Suddenly there was a tremendous crash.

The pirates had fired Long Tom, their big gun. The blast blew Peter far out to sea, and blew Wendy upwards, with only Tinkerbell in John's hat to keep her company. Michael and John found themselves alone in the darkness.

A fairy can be bad as well as good and Tinkerbell was jealous of Wendy.

"Follow me," Tinkerbell said sweetly, "and all will be well!"

The Island Come True

There was a lot of excitement on Neverland. The pirates were looking for the Lost Boys and the redskins were looking for the pirates. A crocodile was looking for Captain Hook, the pirate leader. It had eaten his hand long ago and now it wanted the rest of him. But the crocodile had accidentally swallowed a clock which ticked inside him. Hook always heard the crocodile coming and could escape.

The Lost Boys waited for Peter in their secret underground house. Suddenly Captain Hook accidentally sat on their mushroom chimney and discovered where they lived. But before Hook could do a thing he heard a tick! tick! tick! tick! It was the crocodile! Hook ran off as fast as he could, followed by his men.

The Lost Boys came out of their house. They noticed a great, white bird flying towards them. Tinkerbell flew next to it.

"As it flies it moans 'Poor Wendy'," said Nibs. "It must be a Wendy bird."

"Peter says kill the Wendy bird!" called Tinkerbell.

Peter's orders were always obeyed. Tootles fired an arrow and Wendy fluttered to the ground with the arrow in her breast.

The Lost Boys looked at Wendy.

"It's not a bird. It's a lady," they whispered.

Then they heard Peter's crow. He had arrived home.

"Great news, Boys! I have brought a mother for you all."

Then Peter saw Wendy. He would have killed Tootles for harming her, but something stopped him.

"The Wendy lady! She moves! She lives!" cried Nibs.

Peter knelt beside Wendy. The arrow had struck the acorn button he had given her. It had saved her life.

"Tink is crying because Wendy lives," said Curly.

"Be gone from me forever!" cried Peter when he knew what Tink had done. Only when Wendy pleaded for Tink did Peter change his mind.

"Well, not forever, but for a whole week," he said.

The Lost Boys wanted to carry Wendy to the underground house, but Peter said they must build a new house around her. When John and Michael arrived, they were ordered to help.

When the house was finished, Peter knocked on the door and Wendy came out.

"Oh, Wendy lady, be our mother," said the Lost Boys.

"Very well," said Wendy. "I will do my best."

The boys came into the underground house by sliding through a hollow tree. Everyone had their own tree. One of the first things Peter did was to measure Wendy, John and Michael for their hollow trees. Wendy looked after the boys. Every night she told them a story.

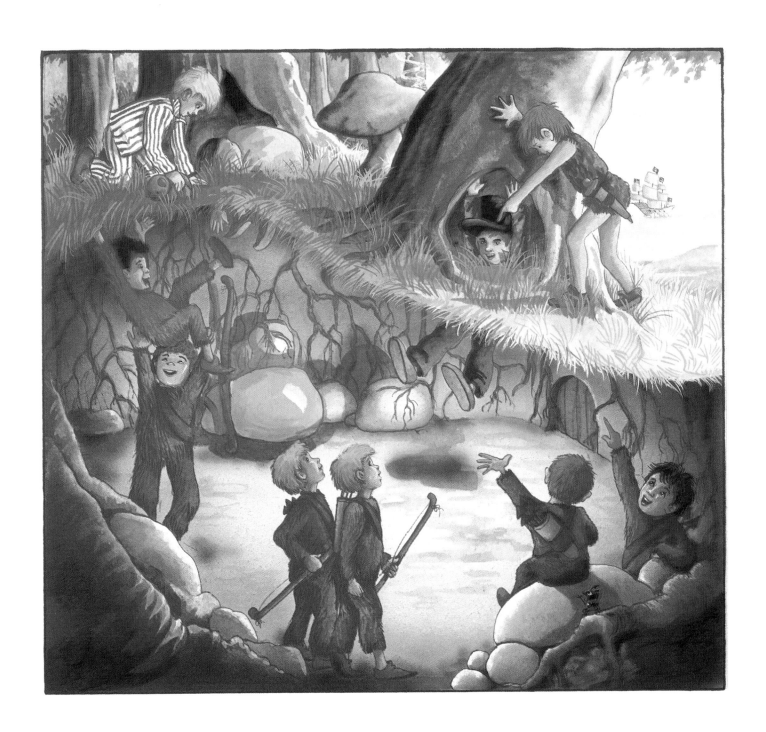

The Mermaids' Lagoon

One evening they were all at the Mermaids' Lagoon sitting on Marooners' Rock. Suddenly Peter sprang to his feet.

"I hear pirates," he said. "Dive!"

They all dived into the water.

A boat with two pirates in drew near to the rock. They had captured Tiger Lily, the redskin princess. They were going to leave her on Marooners' Rock to drown as the tide came in.

"Set her free!" ordered Peter in Captain Hook's voice.

The pirates couldn't see Hook, but they obeyed the voice. They set Tiger Lily free and she swam away.

"Boat ahoy!" Now it really WAS Hook. He was swimming towards the pirates.

"Those boys have found a mother!" he said.

"Could we kidnap her?" asked the pirates.

"Yes, and then we'll take the boys to the ship and make them walk the plank. Then Wendy can be OUR mother," said Hook.

Peter had been listening to the pirates. When he heard Hook ask where Tiger Lily was, Peter was so pleased with what he had done he crowed, and gave himself away.

"Take him! Dead or alive!" shouted Hook.

Hook clambered onto the rock. He caught Peter with his iron hand. Then just as Peter thought his end had come, Hook began to swim wildly towards the pirate ship. He had heard the tick! tick! tick! tick! of the crocodile.

The Lost Boys had gone home. They thought Peter and Wendy were flying on ahead. But they were still on Marooners' Rock, with the water creeping higher and higher.

Peter was injured. He couldn't fly. Wendy wanted to stay with him, but Peter tied the tail of Michael's kite around her waist and she was carried out of sight.

Peter stood on the rock and bravely waited to die.

The Never Bird

Peter could see something moving on the lagoon. It was the Never Bird sitting on her nest. She was trying very hard to paddle towards him.

Neither of them could understand each other's language. But finally Peter saw that she wanted him to take her nest and use it as a boat. Peter then made her a new nest from a hat. She floated off across the lagoon, and Peter headed for home.

Wendy's Story

Since Peter and the Lost Boys had saved Tiger Lily, the redskins had become their friends. They kept guard above the underground house.

One evening when the boys were all in bed, Wendy told them the story they loved best, but Peter hated most.

Wendy's story was about Mr. and Mrs. Darling and their children, and how Nana had been chained up. The children had flown away, and their mother had left the window open for the children to fly back in.

On this night the story made John and Michael want to go home. Wendy wanted to go home too.

"Peter, will you help us?" asked Wendy, not thinking how Peter might feel.

"Yes!" said Peter as if he didn't care. But he did care very much indeed.

Peter said he would ask the redskins to guide Wendy and her brothers through the wood, and he asked Tinkerbell to take them across the sea.

The Lost Boys decided to go with Wendy. Peter said they could go if they wanted to, but HE wasn't going.

Soon all the goodbyes had been said. They began to follow Tinkerbell up the hollow trees. Suddenly the pirates attacked the redskins who were on guard up above.

"Peter! Tell us what to do!" cried the boys.

They waited for the sound of battle to stop.

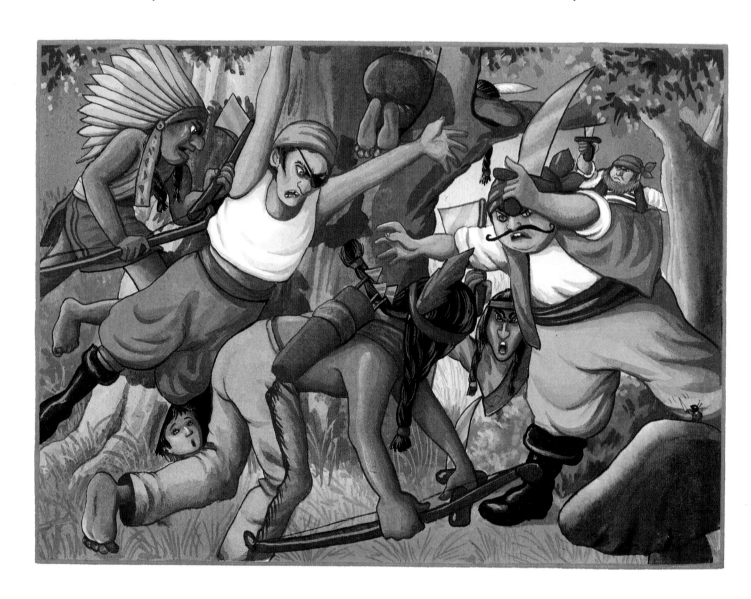

The pirate attack had been a surprise and the redskins were quickly beaten. But it was not the redskins the pirates had come for. It was Peter, Wendy and the Lost Boys.

Hook signalled to a pirate to beat the redskins' tom-tom.

"Hurrah!" said the boys. "The redskins have won!"

They said their goodbyes to Peter again.

Above ground, Hook and his men waited.

Do You Believe in Fairies?

As the boys and Wendy appeared above ground, they were caught and put into Wendy's house. Then the pirates lifted the house onto their shoulders and carried it off.

Hook slid down a hollow tree into the underground house. Peter was on his bed. Hook put poison into Peter's medicine cup then crept away.

Tinkerbell came back to tell Peter the pirates had captured Wendy and the boys.

"I'll rescue them!" Peter cried. He decided to take his medicine first. As he lifted the cup, Tinkerbell quickly drank the medicine herself. She knew that Hook had poisoned it. Peter saw that Tinkerbell was dying.

"If all the children believed in fairies, I would not die," sighed Tinkerbell.

It was night-time. Peter called to all the children who might be dreaming of Neverland.

"If you believe in fairies," he shouted, "clap your hands. Don't let Tinkerbell die!"

Children all over the world clapped. Tinkerbell was saved. Now it was time to save Wendy and the boys.

The Pirate Ship

On the pirate ship the boys were lined up in front of Hook.

"Six of you must walk the plank tonight. But I have room for two cabin boys. Which of you will they be?"

Nobody wanted to be a pirate.

"Get a plank ready!" said Hook. "Fetch their mother."

The pirates tied Wendy to the mast.

Tick! tick! tick! tick!

Everyone heard it. Hook fell into a heap on the deck and crawled away to find a hiding place.

The boys ran to the side of the ship to take a look at the crocodile. There was no crocodile. It was Peter pretending. He signalled to them not to give him away. He pulled himself on board and vanished into a cabin.

The ticking had stopped.

"The crocodile has gone," said one of the pirates.

Hook came out of his hiding place.

Suddenly there was a terrible crowing in one of the cabins. Wendy and the boys knew it was Peter, but the pirates were afraid. They pushed the boys into the cabin to fight whatever was in there.

Peter managed to creep from the cabin and cut the ropes that bound Wendy. Then he took her place at the mast. He took a great breath and crowed his loudest.

Hook made a rush for the figure at the mast. He came face to face with Peter. His last moment had come. There was no escape. Hook jumped into the sea, straight into the jaws of the waiting crocodile.

Now at last the children could fly home.

The Return Home

Mr. Darling had been very sorry when the children flew away. He blamed himself for keeping Nana in the backyard. He crawled into Nana's kennel, and he promised he would never leave it until his children came home.

He stayed in the kennel for a long time. He went to work in it (it had to be specially carried in a taxi-cab). He ate in it. He became quite famous in it.

One evening as Mrs. Darling was playing the nursery piano, Peter and Tinkerbell flew through the open window.

"Quick, Tink!" whispered Peter. "Close the window so they can't get in. Then Wendy will come back with me."

But then he saw Mrs. Darling rest her head on her arms and weep.

"Come on, Tink," he said. "We don't want any silly mothers anyway." And away he flew.

And so it was that when Wendy, John, Michael and the Lost Boys arrived at the window, they found it open.

"Let's slip into our bed. When Mother comes in it will seem as if we've never been away," said Wendy.

At first, Mrs. Darling thought she was dreaming. But when Wendy, John and Michael slipped out of bed and ran into her arms, she knew they were real.

When Wendy Grew Up

Wendy saw Peter once more before he flew away. She told him her parents were going to adopt the Lost Boys, and that they would adopt him too. But Peter said he was going back to Neverland with Tinkerbell.

Mrs. Darling said Wendy could go to Neverland once a year to do spring-cleaning for Peter. Sometimes Peter remembered to come for Wendy and sometimes he forgot. And then Wendy was all grown-up and Peter came no more.

Years passed and Wendy had a daughter of her own called Jane. One day the nursery window was left open and Peter flew in. He cried when he saw that Wendy had grown up. His sobs woke Jane.

"I came to take my mother to Neverland," he said.

"I know," said Jane. "I've been waiting for you."

It was Jane's turn to be Peter's mother. One day Jane will have a daughter, and the story will go on and on.

J. M. Barrie donated the rights to Peter Pan to Great Ormond Street
Children's Hospital in 1929, and to this day the Hospital continues
to benefit from royalties from this generous gift.

ISBN 1 85854 603 6
Published by Brimax Books Ltd, Newmarket, England, CB8 7AU, 1998.
Printed in Spain.